The
Best Detective

"If you're all such great detectives," Jenny March said, "help me find another pass for *Star Quest 2*."

"So solve *that* if you're such a super duper incredible detective," Jason Hutchings said to Nancy. "Come on, you have ten seconds."

Nancy shrugged and held on to her blue detective notebook. "I don't need ten seconds because it's not a mystery. You have to learn what a mystery is before you can be a detective."

"I don't need to learn anything," Jason said. "I'd be the best detective if I could just get my hands on one thing."

"What?" Bess asked.

"Nancy's notebook!" Jason yelled as he jerked it out of Nancy's hands.

The Nancy Drew Notebooks

Available from Simon & Schuster

THE NANCY DREW NOTEBOOKS®

#8

The Best Detective

CAROLYN KEENE
ILLUSTRATED BY ANTHONY ACCARDO

Aladdin Paperbacks
New York   London   Toronto   Sydney   Singapore

This book is a work of fiction. Any references to historical events, real people, or real locales are used fictitiously. Other names, characters, places, and incidents are the product of the author's imagination, and any resemblance to actual events or locales or persons, living or dead, is entirely coincidental.

❧ ALADDIN PAPERBACKS
An imprint of Simon & Schuster Children's Publishing Division
1230 Avenue of the Americas, New York, NY 10020
Copyright © 1995 by Simon & Schuster, Inc.
Produced by Mega-Books, Inc.
All rights reserved, including the right of reproduction in whole or in part in any form.
NANCY DREW and THE NANCY DREW NOTEBOOKS are registered trademarks of Simon & Schuster, Inc.
ALADDIN PAPERBACKS and colophon are trademarks of Simon & Schuster, Inc.
The text of this book was set in Excelsior.
Manufactured in the United States of America
First Aladdin Paperbacks edition April 2002
First Minstrel Books edition September 1995
20 19 18 17

ISBN-13: 978-0-671-87952-5
ISBN-10: 0-671-87952-9
0111 OFF

1

A Free Movie

S*tar Quest 2!*" Nancy Drew whispered to Bess Marvin. "Isn't that super wonderful?"

"Super *excellent!*" Bess answered.

It was Friday afternoon and the end of the school week. Ms. Spencer had just made an announcement to her third-grade class. She had twenty-five free passes to a special preview of the movie *Star Quest 2*.

"A friend of mine got the passes," Ms. Spencer said. "I'll give them out when you settle down, class."

Ms. Spencer tried to look stern, but she couldn't help smiling. Her students were too excited to sit still or stop whispering.

1

Jenny March waved her hand in the air. "Ms. Spencer," she said, "is there an extra pass for my cousin Nina? She's coming to visit me this weekend. She loves *Star Quest*."

Ms. Spencer shook her head. "I'm sorry, Jenny," she said. "I was given just one pass for each of my students."

The school bell rang.

"Line up for the passes," Ms. Spencer said. "And don't forget—the movie is at four-thirty on Sunday afternoon at the River Heights Cinema." She glanced out the window and added, "Please hurry home. I didn't expect rain today, but now it looks as if we might have a storm."

As the class filed out of the room, Ms. Spencer gave each student a movie pass. The passes were small cards with a purple border.

Nancy and Bess waited near their cubbies for another classmate, George Fayne. Then the three best friends hurried down the crowded hallway.

George's real name was Georgia. She

and Bess were cousins. But they looked very different. George was tall with dark curly hair. Bess was shorter and had long blond hair.

Nancy was taller than Bess and shorter than George. She wore her straight reddish blond hair long.

"I can't wait to see *Star Quest 2*," Bess said. "I wish it were Sunday right now."

"Me, too," Nancy said. "I love the first movie. I've seen it a zillion times on video."

"If the new one is just half as good, it will be *great*," George said. "And we get to see it a week before the regular opening!"

Along with all the other students, the girls left the building. They started walking across the schoolyard. Friday afternoons were always noisy. Everyone was laughing and shouting.

Nancy took a close look at her special movie pass. "Wow, I just noticed something," she said. "Our movie passes are like *Star Quest* trading cards. There's a

3

different character on the back of each one. I have star-fighter pilot Zyle. George has the robot dog RFF."

"Ha!" Bess said. She waved her pass at Nancy. "I have my favorite character—Kema, the android."

"Brrr," George said. "It's gotten a lot colder." She shivered in her red sweatshirt.

Bess stopped walking and began to button up her jacket. A strong gust of wind whipped around the girls.

"Arghh!" Bess screamed. "My pass!"

The wind had torn Bess's pass out of her hand. Nancy quickly stuffed her own pass into the pocket of her pants and dashed after Bess's. George did the same. Bess starting running, too. The girls chased the pass all the way across the schoolyard. Each time they came near it, another gust of wind snatched it away.

"Oh, no!" Nancy said. "It's starting to rain."

The first large drops quickly turned into a downpour. Almost everyone in

the schoolyard raced for cover. Some students dashed back to the school building.

George made a running jump and landed on Bess's pass. "I've got it!" she yelled.

"Great!" Nancy said. "Let's get out of the rain. We can go to the Bell."

The girls ran toward the small store that stood by itself next to the schoolyard. The store windows displayed school supplies, toys, and candy. The red, white, and blue sign over the door read The School Bell.

A man with light brown hair and glasses held the door open. He owned the Bell. His name was Charles Pitt, but everyone called him Charlie.

"Come one, come all," Charlie called. "Just be careful not to slip on the wet floor." His blue eyes twinkled with laughter as the dripping kids crowded inside.

Nancy, Bess, and George squeezed into the shop with the other students who had run there to get out of the

6

rain. Like everyone else, they were laughing and trying to catch their breath.

Nancy looked around. She loved the Bell. The counters and shelves were made of dark wood, and the wood floor was polished. An old-fashioned fan hung from the ceiling. Nancy's father used to come to the School Bell when he was a boy. Charlie Pitt's grandfather had run it then.

"I've never seen so many kids in here," Nancy said to Bess and George. "We're like sardines in a can."

"Sardines?" George said. "That's gross."

The girls squirmed past the cash register. They pushed forward until they reached the middle of the store. They stopped near a display rack that held paper clips, rolls of tape, colored pencils, and markers. It was too crowded to go farther.

"Ouch!" Bess cried. "Someone stepped on my toe."

"Not true," a boy in front of her said.

It was Jason Hutchings. He and a few other students from Ms. Spencer's class were standing near the shelves. "You put your toe right under my foot. *Right* under it."

"You're *wrong* as usual," Bess answered.

"Whew!" Nancy said. She pushed her dripping bangs off her forehead. Then she reached into the pocket of her pants and took out her movie pass. "Yuck," she muttered. "It's almost as wet as I am."

"Look at my pass," Bess said, holding up a dirty, limp card. "George really mashed it."

"Yeah, but at least I kept it from blowing away," George said.

"I'm going to put mine inside my notebook," Nancy said. "Then it will dry flat." She took off her backpack, unzipped it, and pulled out a small notebook with a shiny blue cover.

"Can you put mine in, too?" Bess asked.

"Mine, too," George said.

Nancy took their passes. She stuck all three of them between blank pages in the middle of the notebook.

"Ooooh," Jason teased Nancy. "The famous notebook of the world's greatest detective."

"You just wish you could be a great detective like Nancy," George said to Jason.

Nancy loved to solve mysteries. She was good at it, too. Her father had given her the blue notebook. In it she wrote about suspects and clues.

"I could be a detective if I wanted to be," Jason told George. "And I'd be better than Nancy. I'd be the best detective!"

Another classmate, Brenda Carlton, joined the conversation. "You don't need to be a detective to solve mysteries," she said. "Newspaper reporters like me solve mysteries all the time."

Brenda had her own newspaper, *The Carlton News*. She wrote it herself and handed it out at school. Her father was a newspaper publisher. He helped

Brenda design it on their home computer.

"If you're all such great detectives, help me," Jenny March said. "I've got to find another pass for *Star Quest 2*. If I don't, I'll miss the movie." The rain had soaked Jenny's short dark hair. Even her eyelashes were dripping wet. She did *not* look happy.

"Why?" Nancy asked.

"My cousin Nina is coming from Chicago to visit me," Jenny explained. "It's her birthday. My mom will never let me go to the movie without Nina."

"So solve *that* if you're such a super duper incredible detective," Jason said to Nancy. "Come on, you have ten seconds."

Nancy shrugged. "I don't need ten seconds because it's not a mystery. You have to learn what a mystery is before you can be a detective."

"I don't need to learn anything," Jason said. "I'd be the best detective if I could just get my hands on one thing."

"What?" Bess asked.

"That notebook!" Jason yelled as he jerked it out of Nancy's hands. "Ha! I—"

Nancy moved quickly. Before Jason could finish his sentence, she grabbed back the notebook. She unzipped her backpack again. As she stuffed the notebook inside, lightning flashed in the windows of the Bell. Thunder shook the building.

Suddenly the lights went out!

2

In the Dark

Ouch! That was my ear!'' someone yelled.

"Sorry, I thought it was the door handle," a voice answered. "I can't see anything."

The storm clouds blotted out the late afternoon sun. The sky was dark. With all the electric lights out, it seemed like night inside the Bell.

"Okay, kids, don't panic," Charlie Pitt shouted. "Just stand still. The lights will be on before you know it . . . I hope."

"I just bumped into someone," Nancy said. "Was that you, Bess? George?"

A girl answered, "It was me—Jenny. Is this you, Nancy?"

A boy said, "No! it's Jason. And quit pushing!"

"Sorry," Jenny said. "I'll move back."

"Not this way," Nancy said. "There's a display stand. You'll tip it ov—"

Nancy's warning came too late. There was a loud noise.

"Help!" Bess screamed.

Nancy heard a crash and shrieks. She took a step forward and tripped over someone's leg. She flung out her arms to catch herself and landed half on the wood floor and half on someone else.

"Is anyone hurt?" Charlie shouted. "Please, everyone be quiet so I can find out if everyone's okay."

There was silence for a few seconds. Nancy moved her right hand around to find out what was near her. She felt someone's shoulder, a backpack, spilled paper clips, and several pencils.

Charlie Pitt called out, "Everyone stay calm and stand still. Just pretend you're frozen until the lights come on."

Near Nancy's left side someone

began to laugh. "We're not frozen. We're all wet!"

Nancy started to giggle. In a minute everyone heaped on the floor was laughing.

"Who's under me?" Nancy asked when she could speak again.

"I am," George said.

"So am I," Bess said. "At least, I think I am. Ow! who kicked me?"

"I'm just trying to get up," Jason answered.

Suddenly the lights went on.

"Thank goodness!" Charlie said. He hurried over to the fallen display and made sure everyone was all right.

Nancy looked around. Jenny, Brenda, Jason, George, and Bess were brushing themselves off and picking up their things.

The bell on the front door jingled.

"Is Nancy Drew here?" someone called.

Nancy turned and then waved. "Hannah!" she shouted. "I'm over here."

Hannah Gruen was the Drew fami-

ly's housekeeper. She had lived with the Drews since Nancy's mother had died, when Nancy was three years old.

Hannah took a few steps toward Nancy. "My word!" she said. "What happened?"

"It's a mess, but no one's hurt," Charlie Pitt said. "The lights went out. Then a display rack got knocked over."

"When the rain started, I went looking for you in the car," Hannah said to Nancy. "I thought you might come here."

Hannah helped Nancy, Bess, and George gather their belongings. Charlie and several children began setting up the display rack. Others were also picking up school supplies that had fallen on the floor.

"I'll drive you home," Hannah said to Bess and George. "But we've got to hurry. The car is double-parked."

"I can't find my backpack," Nancy said.

"Isn't this one yours?" Brenda asked. She held out a purple pack.

"Yes. Thanks," Nancy said.

Hannah steered the three girls through the crowded shop to the door. "Let's go," she said. "I'm blocking traffic."

Nancy glanced back at the school supplies that were still lying all over the floor. "Sorry about the mess," she said to Charlie.

He winked at her. "The next time the weather report says rain, I'll just keep the Bell closed."

Hannah dropped Bess and George at their houses. Then she drove home with Nancy.

"You'd better get out of those wet clothes right away," Hannah said. "In fact, a hot bath would be a good thing for you."

"Wouldn't hot cocoa be even better?" Nancy asked.

Hannah laughed. "Take a bath, and I promise you'll find cocoa waiting for you."

After her bath and cocoa, Nancy read

a library book until her father came home. Then they had dinner together.

"How's my soggy pumpkin?" Carson Drew asked Nancy. Pumpkin was one of his favorite nicknames for her. "Do you think all the rain today will make you grow round and orange faster?"

Nancy giggled. "I didn't get *that* wet." Then she told her father about her day at school and about the rainstorm. She also told him about the free passes to *Star Quest 2*.

"Sunday afternoon at four-thirty?" Mr. Drew asked. He pretended to frown. "Isn't that when you and Hannah were planning to clean out your closet?"

Nancy laughed at his teasing. "I wouldn't miss this movie for anything," she said. "Especially not for closet cleaning!"

While Nancy was helping to clear the table, George telephoned.

"Are you still coming over tomorrow morning?" George asked. George had promised to show Nancy how to turn and change directions on in-line skates.

"Hannah says I can bike to your house at ten," Nancy replied. "Is Bess coming, too?"

"No," George answered. "She says she doesn't like in-line skating as much as ice skating." Then George asked, "Do you have the movie passes? All three of them?"

"Yes," Nancy said. "They're inside my blue notebook in my backpack."

"Are you sure?" George asked.

"Of course," Nancy said. "I put my notebook away before the lights went out at the Bell. I've left the passes inside so they'll dry flat."

Nancy finished making plans with George and hung up the phone. She decided to check the movie passes. Her backpack was lying on the floor in the front hall.

Nancy unzipped her pack and looked inside. Her heart skipped a beat. She turned the backpack upside down and shook it as hard as she could. Everything fell on the floor.

Nancy gasped. Her notebook was gone!

3

Lost or Stolen?

Nancy stared at the floor. She couldn't believe her eyes.

Mr. Drew walked into the hallway. "What's wrong, Pumpkin?" he asked. "You look as though you've seen a ghost. Or two ghosts. Isn't it too early for Halloween?"

"Daddy!" Nancy cried. "I've lost my blue notebook!"

"Maybe you left it at school," her father said.

Nancy shook her head. "No. I know I had it after school because I put our movie passes inside. They're gone, too!"

Mr. Drew hurried over to Nancy and

put his arm around her. "Tell me everything that happened," he said.

Nancy liked to discuss problems with her father. He was a lawyer and gave her good advice. She described exactly what had taken place in the Bell that afternoon.

"Pumpkin," her father said, "I think there's a good chance you lost your notebook at the Bell. There was a lot of commotion when the lights went out. The notebook might be lying on the floor. Or maybe Charlie or someone else found it already."

"Maybe," Nancy said.

Mr. Drew kissed her on the forehead.

"Let's check the car first to make sure the notebook isn't there. Then you can call the Bell. Maybe Charlie is working late."

Nancy and her father went outside and searched the car. They didn't find the notebook. Then Nancy tried calling the Bell. No one answered.

"You can try again tomorrow morning," Mr. Drew said. "I bet Charlie will have cleaned up the shop and found your notebook by then."

Nancy nodded, but she was still upset. She kept thinking about Bess and George. Missing the movie herself was awful. But making her best friends miss it was much worse.

"I should call Bess and George now," Nancy said.

"Maybe not," Mr. Drew replied. "No one can do anything until tomorrow. You can tell them first thing in the morning. Then they won't be upset all night."

Nancy went up to her room. She put on her nightgown and robe. Then she sat at her desk, going over everything that had happened at the Bell.

She picked up a pencil and tried to do her math homework. But she kept thinking about her missing notebook and the movie passes inside it. Nancy wrote a name on her math worksheet: "Jason."

Maybe he took my notebook, she thought. Maybe he took it when the lights were out and my pack was lying on the floor. He tried to grab the notebook just before that. Maybe he took it to tease me.

Nancy dropped the pencil and ran downstairs to call Jason.

As soon as he answered the phone, Nancy said, "My blue notebook is missing. It had three movie passes in it. So I've got to get the notebook back. Did you see it after the lights went out? Or . . . did you take it?"

"Nope," Jason said. "I didn't see it or touch it after you took it back. Hey, is this a mystery?"

"Yes, and I've got to solve it before four-thirty on Sunday," Nancy said. "If not, Bess, George, and I will miss the movie."

"I'll get your notebook for you," Jason said.

"You will? Do you know where it is?" Nancy asked.

"Not yet," Jason said. "But whoever finds a detective's missing notebook must be the best detective. So if I find

the notebook before you do, then I'm the best detective, right?"

"I never said that," Nancy answered.

"Ha! It's true," Jason said. "It's a fight to the finish. May the best detective win!"

Jason hung up. So did Nancy. She put her hands on her hips. Her father walked into the room.

"What's up, Pumpkin?" he asked.

"I think Jason might have my notebook," Nancy said. Then she told her father all about Jason.

"If he really has your notebook," Mr. Drew said, "everything will work out fine."

Nancy made a face. "He'll pretend to find the notebook. We'll get the movie passes back. But everyone will think *he's* the best detective."

Mr. Drew shook his head. "Don't worry about that. You've solved more than one mystery. You're the real detective. And the best!"

Nancy felt a little better. But she was still worried. She went upstairs and brushed her teeth. That night she had trouble falling asleep.

Nancy awakened early on Saturday morning. The first thing she thought about was the missing notebook and movie passes. She jumped out of bed. After she washed up, she put on comfortable jeans and a purple sweater, and went downstairs. Right after breakfast she called Bess.

"Can you meet me at George's house at ten?" Nancy asked.

"You changed your mind. You don't want to do in-line skating," Bess guessed. "Super! Now we can do something that's fun!"

Nancy was upset, but she still laughed. "Well, that's not exactly it," she said. "But I'll explain everything."

A few minutes later Nancy got ready to leave. She tucked her math notebook into her backpack. I may need something to write in, she thought.

At exactly ten o'clock Nancy rang George's doorbell. Her heart was beating fast. George opened the door. Bess was with her.

"I've got really bad news," Nancy told her friends as soon as she was inside the house. She took a deep breath and spoke as fast as she could. "My blue notebook is missing, and so are the movie passes."

Bess gasped. "The movie passes!"

"Oh, no! What happened?" George asked.

Nancy told her friends everything. Then she said, "I'm sorry. I wish none of this had happened. Are you really mad at me?"

"No," George said.

Bess shook her head. "It's not your fault. Besides, I know you'll find the passes."

"I hope so. I'm going right to the Bell," Nancy said. "Keep your fingers crossed. Maybe Charlie has my notebook."

"I want to go with you," Bess said. "Don't you, George? We could be detectives, too, and help Nancy."

"Definitely!" George said.

Bess and George got permission to bike to the Bell. The girls rode in a single file line with Nancy first. It was just a few blocks to the shop. Nancy kept thinking about her notebook.

Please be there, she thought. Please be at the Bell!

She pedaled faster. The Bell was around the next corner. Nancy got ready to turn.

Suddenly another bike raced around the corner straight at Nancy. There was no time for her to stop.

"Watch out!" George shouted.

4

The Race Is On

Nancy swerved sharply to the left and braked hard. The other rider braked, too. Nancy's back wheel grazed the other bike's front tire. Her bike wobbled. She jumped off just as it fell.

"Nancy, are you all right?" Bess cried.

The other rider was Jason. He dropped his bike and ran over to Nancy. "Are you okay?"

Nancy nodded. "I hope you're detective work is better than your bike riding, Jason," she said to him.

"Jason Hutchings, you ride like a maniac!" George said.

Jason picked up Nancy's bike. "Sorry," he said.

"Have you found out anything about my notebook?" Nancy asked.

"Detectives don't blab information," Jason answered. "Especially not to the competition. My lips are *zipped*."

He moved his thumb and index finger across his lips as if zipping them closed. Then he got on his bike and rode away, shouting, "It's a fight to the finish!"

"I guess his lip zipper is broken," Nancy muttered.

The girls rode around the corner. They parked their bikes in the rack in front of the Bell and went inside. Charlie was wiping the counter next to the cash register.

"Look who's here," he said. "Been out in any good rainstorms lately?"

Nancy laughed but then became serious.

"Yesterday I lost my blue notebook here," she said. "There were three movie passes inside. Did you find it anywhere?"

Charlie stared at Nancy. "I'll bet it had a pocket on the inside, too."

"Yes!" Nancy, Bess, and George shouted.

"How did you know?" Nancy asked.

"A boy just stopped by," Charlie said. "He asked about the same notebook."

"Jason Hutchings!" Bess said.

"He crawled all over the place searching for it," Charlie continued. "I should have thanked him for polishing the floor."

"Did he find anything?" Nancy asked.

"I don't know," Charlie answered. "He left while I was busy at the cash register."

"You didn't find anything when you cleaned up after the storm, did you?" Bess asked.

"Nope," Charlie said. "Sorry."

"If it's okay with you, we'd like to look around for the notebook," Nancy said.

Charlie laughed. "Why not? Let me

31

know if you want to use the mop. We could kill two birds with one stone."

The girls began to look around the shop carefully.

"You can see marks in the dust under the counters," George said. "Zipper Lips must have searched under here."

Bess checked the tops of all the counters. Nancy looked at the shelves. She noticed that Charlie had refilled the overturned display rack. The store looked tidier than ever.

Nancy sighed. "I don't see it. Even if the notebook had been here this morning, I guess Jason would have found it."

The girls said goodbye to Charlie and rode back to George's house.

"I'm not in the mood for skating," George said as they got off their bikes.

"Me either," Nancy said.

"That's one good thing," Bess said.

The girls went to George's bedroom and talked about what to do next. Nancy got out her math notebook and turned to a clean page.

"Okay, detective team," she said,

"let's make a list of suspects. We'll think of everyone who saw me put the notebook in my pack and had a reason to take it."

"Zipper Lips *doesn't* go on the list," George said. "If he took your notebook yesterday, he wouldn't have gone to the Bell to look for it today."

"But he could have found the notebook there this morning," Nancy said. "Maybe he sneaked it out of the Bell and put it in his bike pack. Maybe he's keeping it to tease me." Nancy wrote down Jason's name.

"How about Jenny March?" Bess asked. "She was standing with us. She really wanted another movie pass for her cousin Nina."

"Right," Nancy said as she wrote Jenny's name on the page. "Then there's Brenda Carlton."

"Why Brenda?" George asked.

"She said reporters could solve mysteries," Nancy replied. "Maybe she took the notebook and will pretend to find it. Or maybe she won't give it back.

Maybe she wants to show that I'm not a good detective."

"That would be so mean!" Bess said.

"That would be so *Brenda-ish!*" George said.

Nancy added Brenda's name to the list and shut the notebook. "Let's go look for clues. We can start with Jenny," she said.

The girls got permission from George's mother to bike to Jenny's house. They left their bicycles next to a tall hedge near the Marches' driveway. The driveway ran along one side of the house. The Marches' car was parked in the driveway.

"We have to get close to the house without being seen," Nancy said.

"What are we looking for?" Bess asked.

"Anything that helps," Nancy answered.

The girls tiptoed along the far side of the hedge.

"See all those bushes near the side

35

door of the house?" Nancy whispered. "Let's hide there."

A moment later all three girls were crouched in the bushes next to the March house.

"I'm going to look in that window," Nancy whispered. She pointed to the window right above where they were hiding.

She slowly stood up and placed her hands on the window frame. She stretched up as high as she could on her toes.

"What are you doing?" she heard someone say inside the house.

Nancy gasped and dropped down. The side door to the house swung open. A man stepped out and walked to the car in the driveway.

"I don't know what's taking you all so long," he called back toward the house. "I'm starting the car."

"That's Mr. March," George whispered.

A woman walked out of the house, carrying a large backpack. She got into the car next to Mr. March. She called back to the house, "Jenny! Nina!"

Nancy, Bess, and George heard giggling inside. A moment later Jenny and a girl with short red hair hurried out the door. They each carried a backpack.

"I can't believe we pulled it off, Nina," Jenny said. "You've got a pass to *Star Quest 2!*"

5

Toys and Clues

She got a pa—" Bess started to say.

Nancy clamped a hand over Bess's mouth. "Don't move or say anything," she whispered.

Nancy ran to the side of the Marches' house that was opposite the driveway. Then she ran from the house down to the sidewalk. Jenny and the red-haired girl climbed into the car. As Mr. March backed the car down the driveway, Nancy walked along the sidewalk toward the car.

"Pretty neat!" George whispered. "Nancy looks like she's just walking up the street and happens to see them in the car."

"Jenny!" Nancy called. She waved. "Stop!"

Mr. March put on the brakes. Nancy ran up to the car window.

"Hi," Nancy said to Jenny. "I've got to ask you something. I lost my blue notebook at the Bell yesterday when the lights went out. There were three movie passes inside. Did you see my notebook or pick it up by mistake? You were standing right there."

Jenny shook her head. "Did you go back to the Bell? Maybe it's still there."

"I looked for it at the Bell this morning," Nancy said. She quickly glanced at the backpacks in the car. She was hoping for a clue of some sort. "I didn't find anything."

"Girls," Mr. March said, "I'm sorry to cut this off, but we've got to get going. We won't have much of a hike at the state park unless we leave right now."

Jenny waved to Nancy as the car backed into the street. When it turned the corner, Nancy motioned Bess and George to come out.

"What did she say?" Bess asked.

"Not much," Nancy answered. "She just asked if I'd been back to the Bell."

"Jenny March!" George said. "I always thought she was nice. But she must have taken your notebook. How else could she have gotten a movie pass for her cousin?"

Nancy nodded. "That's what I think, too. And now she's gone for the day."

Bess groaned. "We're stuck until she gets back, and the movie is tomorrow!"

"We'd better investigate the other suspects," Nancy said. "You never know what might come up." She glanced at her watch. "Uh-oh! I've got to get home for lunch."

"I have an idea," Bess said. "Come with me and my mom to the toy fair at the mall this afternoon. I heard Brenda say that she's going. We could talk to her there."

"Okay," Nancy said. "George, too?"

George shook her head. "I have to go to the dentist. Maximum yuck."

The girls finished making plans and got their bikes. As Nancy rode home, she kept thinking, How could Jenny do something so awful? And how can we get the passes back?

Hannah made one of Nancy's favorite sandwiches—tuna salad with tomato. While Nancy ate it, she asked if she could go to the toy fair with Bess. Hannah said yes.

An hour after lunch Mrs. Marvin picked Nancy up and drove her and Bess to the mall. She walked the girls inside. Half of the main court was filled with colorful display booths overflowing with toys. People strolled along the aisles between the booths.

"Stay in this part of the court," Mrs. Marvin said. "Then you can walk around the fair by yourselves."

The girls started up the main aisle.

"Oooh, check out all the new *Star Quest* toys!" Bess said. "Let's look at

41

them. Oh, I love the Kema android doll."

"This is really neat, too," Nancy said. "An RFF robot dog that runs on batteries."

The girls looked at the stuffed animals next. Then Bess stopped at the doll display. Nancy walked on to find the watercolor sets.

"Isn't this a strange place to look for your notebook?" a familiar voice said.

Nancy turned around. Brenda Carlton was standing behind her.

"How did you know my notebook is missing?" Nancy asked.

"I heard the terrible news from Jason Hutchings," Brenda said. "I was going to write an important article for the *Carlton News* about the toy fair. But now I think I'll do a story about how a detective lost her notebook—and movie passes."

Brenda flipped open a red notebook. "How do you, Bess, and George feel about missing the *Star Quest 2* preview?" she asked.

"Maybe we won't miss it," Nancy said.

Brenda smiled. She looked as if she didn't believe Nancy. "Are Bess and George super angry at you for losing the passes?" she asked.

"As a matter of fact, they're not," Nancy answered.

Brenda shook her head as if she didn't believe Nancy. She wrote something in her red notebook. Then she said, "Here's my last question. If Jason finds your notebook, will you admit to the *News* that he's the best detective?"

"The only thing I'll admit now is this—I plan to find that notebook," Nancy said. "*And* the passes."

"I hope you can," Brenda said. She put her own notebook away. "Because everyone else is going to the preview— even Jenny March's cousin."

"Where did Jenny get an extra pass for her cousin?" Nancy asked. "Do you know?"

"Isn't that the kind of question a detective is supposed to answer?" Brenda

said with a mean smile. "Especially the *best* detective. 'Bye."

Brenda turned and walked away.

She knows something I don't know, Nancy thought. Are she and Jenny both in on it? Then Nancy saw Bess hurrying toward her.

"There you are," Bess said.

"I just talked to Brenda," Nancy said. "She knows that Jenny found a pass for her cousin. But she won't say anything else."

"Do you think Jenny and Brenda planned this with each other?" Bess asked. "Do you think there's a . . . what-do-you-call-it?"

"A conspiracy," Nancy said. "Maybe. I need some time to think about all this."

Mrs. Marvin drove Nancy home in the late afternoon. Nancy went right to her room. She sat on her bed and opened her math notebook.

Jenny, Brenda, and Jason, she thought. Three different suspects? Or one thief and two helpers? Maybe Jenny didn't take the notebook. Maybe Jason or Brenda took it to prove I'm not the best detective. Either of them could have given Jenny an extra pass.

I'm stuck, Nancy thought, until I find out if Jenny's extra pass is one of ours.

Nancy drew a big question mark in her math notebook. I know what to do next, she thought. I'll tell Jenny that I heard she got another pass. I'll ask her where she got it because George, Bess, and I need new ones.

Nancy jumped off her bed and ran downstairs. She telephoned Jenny's house.

A woman answered. "Hello?"

"May I speak to Jenny?" Nancy asked.

"I'm sorry," the woman said. "She won't be back until very late tonight."

Nancy sighed. "Okay, I'll call tomorrow morning. Thanks. 'Bye."

Nancy telephoned George and explained her plan to talk to Jenny the next morning.

"Why don't we all go over to her house?" George said. "We could meet there at ten."

"Sure," Nancy said. "Call Bess, okay?"

At dinner Nancy told her father everything that had happened that day.

"I think you're right about the next step," Mr. Drew said. "Talk to Jenny." Then he added, "You look like one glum pumpkin."

"I'm afraid I won't find the passes," Nancy said. "There's not much time left."

After dinner Nancy didn't feel like playing. She read until bedtime. She washed up and got under the covers as fast as she could. She wanted morning to come soon.

When Nancy opened her eyes, the sun was shining. She felt just as rushed as she had the night before. She put on jeans and a red sweater and was in the kitchen before Hannah. After breakfast Nancy got ready to leave. At 9:45 she stood with her bike on the sidewalk near Jenny's house.

Suppose the Marches go out while I wait for Bess and George? she thought.

Too worried to wait, Nancy walked her bike up to the porch. She rang the doorbell. Mr. March opened the door.

"May I talk to Jenny?" Nancy asked.

"Sure," Mr. March answered. "She's upstairs. Come in and I'll get her."

Nancy stepped into the entry hallway. Mr. March started up the stairs. Nancy glanced around. The house was very quiet.

Nancy rested her arm on a low marble-topped table in the hall. A glass vase stood in the center of the table. She noticed the corners of something sticking out from under the vase. Cards with purple borders, Nancy thought. Two *Star Quest 2* passes!

Quietly and carefully, Nancy lifted the edge of the vase. She reached for the passes.

"Hey, what are you doing? Those aren't yours!" someone screamed. "Thief!"

6

She Didn't Do It!

Nancy pulled her hand away from the passes and whirled around. Jenny's cousin Nina was standing in the kitchen door. Mr. March and Jenny came running down the stairs.

"What's going on?" Mr. March asked.

Nina pointed to Nancy. "She was about to steal our *Star Quest 2* passes!"

"I wasn't stealing them," Nancy said. "I was just going to look at them." Nancy turned to Jenny. "I heard you got an extra pass. I wanted to know where you got it because mine is missing and so are Bess's and George's. Ms. Spencer said there weren't any extra ones."

"Emily Reeves can't go to the movie," Jenny explained. "Her grandmother in Detroit got sick. Emily and her mom went to visit her in the hospital. Emily told Brenda yesterday morning, and Brenda called me. Nina and I went to get Emily's ticket right away."

Nina nodded. She looked embarrassed. "I'm sorry I called you a thief," she said to Nancy. "I didn't know what you were doing."

"That's okay," Nancy said.

"I'm sorry your passes got lost," Jenny said to Nancy. "If I couldn't go to the movie, I'd give you my pass. I really would."

"Of course you would," Mr. March said.

"Thanks, Jenny," Nancy said, opening the door. "See you later—or tomorrow."

Nancy walked her bike to the corner.

I'm glad Jenny isn't a thief, she thought. But where is my notebook? What happened to our passes?

As soon as Bess and George arrived, Nancy told them about Nina's pass.

"Well, Jenny wasn't in a plot with Brenda," George said. "Now what do we do?"

"We're *not* giving up," Nancy said. "Let's find out what Jason's been up to."

"Zipper Lips?" Bess asked. She made a face.

"Yes," Nancy said. "If he's been doing detective work, maybe he knows something. If he took the notebook, maybe we'll find a way to get it back. Let's call him now."

Bess looked at her watch. "I can't. My grandma is taking me to the mall. I want to show her the Kema android doll. You know, just in case she ever needs a present idea for someone."

"I told my mom I'd help rake leaves," George said. "But it won't take long."

"I'll start tracking Jason down," Nancy said. "Then I'll call you."

Nancy rode home. Just six hours to go, she thought. Maybe Jason has some ideas. Maybe he'll work with us. Maybe four heads are better than three—even if one head is Jason's.

Nancy telephoned Jason's house as soon as she got home. His mother answered.

"Is Jason there?" Nancy asked. "I'm in his class at school. My name's Nancy Drew."

"He's at a Little League playoff game in the park," Mrs. Hutchings answered. "Do you want to leave a message?"

"No, thanks," Nancy said. " 'Bye."

Nancy found her father in his study. "May I ride my bike to the park?" she asked.

Mr. Drew glanced at the clock. "Yes, but be back for lunch," he said. "And watch the traffic light on the corner near the park."

"I will and I will," Nancy said. "Two 'I wills' equals 'I really will.' "

Her father laughed and waved goodbye.

Nancy got to the park quickly on her bike. A crowd of cheering people stood around the fence behind home plate. Jason's team was at bat.

"What's the score?" Nancy asked a teenage girl.

"It's tied, and the game is almost over," the girl said. "But if the team at bat scores, they'll win."

Nancy walked her bike to where Jason's team was standing. Mike Minelli, Jason's best friend, was getting ready to bat.

Nancy leaned her bike against a tree. Then she tapped Jason on the shoulder and asked, "Can I talk to you for a minute? It's really important. It's about my missing notebook."

"I'm playing ball now," Jason said. "I can't do detective work at the same time. I may be the best, but I'm not superhuman—yet." Then he yelled at Mike, "Hit a home run!"

The pitcher threw the ball. Mike swung and missed. Strike one.

"Just tell me if you have any clues," Nancy said. "Please! Time is running out."

"Ha! I'm not telling my best detective secrets," Jason said.

The pitcher threw the ball. Again Mike swung and missed. Strike two.

"This is an emergency," Nancy said. "I don't want my friends to miss the movie."

Jason looked at Nancy. His face became serious. "Guess what?" he whispered.

"What?" Nancy asked.

Jason laughed. "I haven't got a clue!"

Nancy made a face. "Come on, Jason. Did you notice—" she started to ask.

Jason had turned back to the game. The pitcher threw the ball. Mike swung hard. Wham! The ball shot past the shortstop. An outfielder dashed for it and missed.

"Home run! Go home!"

Nancy found herself shouting along with everyone else. Mike raced around second base, around third, and across home plate.

"We won!" Jason yelled. "Yahoooo!" He and the rest of the team ran toward Mike.

Nancy watched the team members

55

and their fans cheer and clap. After a few minutes the crowd broke up. Nancy saw Jason, Mike, and Mr. Minelli walk out of the park toward a car and get into it. The car started to pull away from the curb.

So much for that angle, Nancy thought.

Then the car stopped and backed up to the curb. Mike jumped out and sprinted back to the baseball field.

"What's up, Minelli?" the coach asked. "Are you back for another game?"

"Nope," Mike said. "Jason and I forgot our gym bags."

Mike hurried to a spot close to where Nancy stood. Several players and their families were milling around. Mike bent down to grab the handles of two canvas bags.

"Hey, Mike," the coach said. "This jacket has Jason's name in it." He handed Mike a green-and-white windbreaker.

"Yep, that's his," Mike replied. He

unzipped one of the bags and pulled it open wide. Just before he stuffed the jacket inside, Nancy saw something lying on top.

It was rectangular, blue, and shiny.

Nancy gasped. "That's my notebook!"

7

The Blue Notebook

Nancy froze. She felt as though the wind had been knocked out of her. Mike snatched the two bags and started running. He left Jason's bag unzipped.

"Mike!" Nancy shouted.

The coach shouted Mike's name in the same instant. His deep voice drowned Nancy's out. Mike turned his head.

"Good game!" the coach yelled.

Mike smiled and kept running. Nancy dashed to the tree where she had left her bike. By the time she was pedaling to the edge of the park, Mr. Minelli's car had pulled away.

I'll catch them at the traffic light, Nancy thought.

She raced her bike along the sidewalk. In the street, the car was moving faster. As it reached the corner, the light changed to yellow. Nancy pedaled as hard as she could. The car crossed the intersection. Nancy reached the corner. The light turned red.

"Rats!" she muttered as she braked. She watched the car disappear down the street.

Why did Jason lie to me? Nancy wondered. Does he plan to give back the notebook at the last minute? Is he going somewhere with Mike Minelli? Or is he going home? Suppose he loses his gym bag. Suppose my notebook falls out of it!

The light changed. Nancy walked her bike across the street.

I'll phone Jason as soon as I get home, she thought. I'll tell him what I saw and make him give back my notebook.

She looked at her watch. It was noon.

Nancy rode home quickly. She went straight to the kitchen to make her call.

Jason's mother answered the phone again.

"May I talk to Jason?" Nancy asked. "This is Nancy Drew. I called before."

"Oh, right," Mrs. Hutchings said. "Jason is having lunch with Mike Minelli. But he should be home by about one-thirty. Why don't you call back then?"

"Do you know where he's having lunch?" Nancy asked. "It's really important."

"Mr. Minelli took them to a restaurant," Mrs. Hutchings answered. "But I don't know which one. I can have him call you as soon as he gets in."

Nancy said goodbye to Mrs. Hutchings and called George.

"Gigantic news," Nancy said. "My notebook is in Jason Hutchings's gym bag."

"You mean he's had it all this time?" George said. "Did you get the passes?"

"I didn't get anything yet," Nancy said. She explained what had happened. "Can you and Bess meet me in

60

front of Jason's house a little before one-thirty?"

"Sure," George said. "Just think about it—in Zipper Lips' gym bag. That's so gross."

When Nancy got off the phone, she helped her father set the table for lunch. He had made tomato soup and cheese sandwiches.

"Well, well, well—it's the bicycling detective," Carson Drew said. "You've had a busy morning. How's the case going?"

"I might be close to solving it," Nancy said. "But it's pretty weird." She told her father about Jason and the gym bag.

Mr. Drew frowned. "That's mean if he's had your notebook and hasn't returned it. When are you getting it back?"

"I want to go over to his house after lunch," Nancy said. "George says she and Bess can meet me there."

When they finished eating, Nancy and her father cleared the table. Then she biked to Jason's house. She sat on one of the porch steps, waiting. A few minutes later Bess and George arrived. They sat on the lower steps.

"Incredible," George said. "Jason tells you he hasn't found out anything about your notebook. Meanwhile the notebook is lying in his gym bag. How can a person do something like that?"

"Maybe he's not a person," Nancy said. "Maybe he's an evil android—like Thurtik in the first *Star Quest* movie."

Bess sighed. "Do you think the passes will smell like Jason's gym bag?"

Nancy and George burst out laughing. They were still giggling when Mr. Minelli's car pulled up.

"Here we go," Nancy whispered.

Jason got out of the car with his gym bag. He waved goodbye to Mike and started up the walk to his house. Then he noticed the girls sitting on the front steps of his house. They all stared at him.

"It's my fan club!" Jason said. He

gave them a big grin. "I bet you've been waiting hours for my autograph."

"We've been waiting more than a day for you to give back my notebook," Nancy said in an angry tone.

"I already told you," Jason said. "I have *zero*. No clues, no notebook, nothing."

Bess jumped up. "That's a big lie!"

"It is *not!*" Jason said.

"You have my notebook in your gym bag," Nancy said. "I saw it there in the park."

Jason looked puzzled. Then he turned red. "Oh, that," he muttered. He unzipped his gym bag and took out a notebook with a shiny blue cover.

"That's my notebook!" Nancy said.

"Nope, mine," Jason said. "See? It's a new one." He fanned the pages. "All blank."

"Where did you get that?" George asked.

"At the Bell, before the game this morning," Jason answered. "Charlie has all kinds of notebooks. Stacks of them."

The three girls stared silently at the notebook. Then Nancy asked, "Why did you buy a notebook anyway?"

Jason blushed again. "I thought I'd have better luck solving the case if I had a detective's notebook. You know—like you do."

"Sorry," Nancy said. "I guess I jumped to conclusions."

The girls got their bikes. Jason walked up the porch steps. Before he went inside, he said, "Too bad no one has solved this case." Then he grinned. "Yet."

"What do we do now?" George asked.

"It's two o'clock," Nancy said, "and I'm out of ideas. I feel really bad. Because of me you're going to miss the movie."

"My parents said they'd take us to another movie this afternoon," Bess said. "But I'm not sure I feel like it."

Nancy and George both shook their

heads. They didn't want to see just any movie. They wanted to see *Star Quest 2*.

The girls said goodbye. None of them was smiling.

When Nancy got home, she told her father about the conversation with Jason.

Mr. Drew put his arm around Nancy. "I'm sorry about the movie preview. The minute *Star Quest 2* opens, I'll take you girls to see it. I promise."

"Thanks, Daddy," Nancy said.

"What can I do now to cheer you up?" Mr. Drew asked. "Strawberry ice cream with half a can of chocolate sauce? Twelve games of dominoes? Should I sing?"

"Don't sing!" Nancy said. She put her hands over her ears. She tried to laugh but couldn't. "I know what I want to do—watch my videotape of the first *Star Quest* movie."

"Good idea," Mr. Drew said. "One more time and we'll both know it by heart."

Nancy and her father made a big

bowl of popcorn. They went into the family room to watch the tape.

The title of the movie appeared on the screen: *Star Quest*. In just two hours, *Star Quest 2* will begin, Nancy thought. She tried to pay attention to the video, but it was hard.

Star-fighter pilot Zyle was reprogramming RFF, the robot dog.

"I want you to fetch the newspaper on my computer screen every morning," Zyle said, "like a good robot dog. I don't want you to sit at my desk and read the whole thing."

Nancy laughed. Little by little she forgot everything except the movie in front of her. The minutes slipped by.

"Here comes a funny part," Nancy said to her father.

Zyle's star-fighter ship was nearing the space station. A message from the fleet commander came over the ship's communication system. "All star fighters. There's a twenty-minute wait to get into the docking bay."

"It's a total traffic jam," Zyle said to

co-pilot Kema. "Fourteen ships stacked up like pancakes. Like pancakes, I tell you! I feel like a lump of butter in the middle of the stack."

Kema stared at Kyle with her bright blue android eyes. "What's a pancake?" she asked.

Nancy started to laugh, then sat up straight. "Wait—" she said. Then she jumped up and stopped the videotape.

"Daddy!" she cried. "You've got to drive me to the Bell. Now!"

8

The Best Detective Wins

Mr. Drew looked puzzled. "What?"

Nancy glanced at her watch. "It's five minutes to four. The Bell closes at four. Daddy, please hurry! I think I've solved the mystery. I'll explain in the car. Please!"

Carson Drew stared at his daughter. Then he stood up and said, "Let's go!"

Nancy ran into the kitchen. "Hannah, can you call Bess and George? Please say I've found the passes. Tell them to be at the River Heights Cinema by 4:25. It's super important! I'll explain later."

Nancy dashed out to the car. Mr.

69

Drew had the motor running. Nancy jumped in. As her father drove down the street, Nancy quickly told him about her hunch. Then she fixed her eyes on the dashboard clock.

One minute to four. Four o'clock. One minute past four. Two minutes past four.

They turned the last corner.

"It's closed!" Nancy cried, seeing the dark windows and the sign on the Bell's door.

She glanced toward the street again. At the end of the block someone was getting into a car. "That's Charlie Pitt! We've got to stop him!"

Carson Drew stepped on the gas just as Charlie's car pulled into the street. Mr. Drew honked his horn—one short blast after another. Charlie didn't stop. Mr. Drew kept honking. He flipped on the flashing lights. At the next corner Charlie stopped.

"Stay here," Nancy's father said as he set the emergency brake. He jumped out and sprinted up to Charlie's car.

Nancy watched them talk. Five minutes past four. Six minutes past four. Mr. Drew hurried back to their car. Charlie turned the corner and drove down the street.

"What happened?" Nancy asked as her father started driving.

"We're just going around the block," Mr. Drew answered. "Charlie says he'll open up the store."

Nine minutes past four. Nancy leaped out of the car as Charlie unlocked the shop door. He switched on the lights.

Nancy ran to the shelves that held paper and notebooks. She searched through a tall pile of notebooks with bright-colored covers and single pockets—red ones, blue ones, purple, orange, green.

"Here it is! Mine!" She held up a blue notebook. "It fell out of my pack when the lights went out. Then it was put on the shelf with the new notebooks. Like a lump of butter in the middle of a stack of pancakes!"

Charlie looked puzzled. "I'm not sure how notebooks are like lumps of butter. But I'm glad you found yours. Are those passes you were looking for inside the notebook?"

Nancy shook her notebook. Three cards fell into her hand. They were faded and dirty, and very flat and dry. Nancy grinned.

"Thank you gazillions for opening the store!" Nancy said to Charlie. "I'll explain everything after school tomorrow."

"It's a deal," he replied. "I won't even charge you for the notebook storage."

Nancy raced out the door and got into the car. At exactly 4:25, Carson Drew pulled up in front of the theater.

"Thanks, Daddy!" Nancy said.

"Good work, Detective Drew," he said. He gave Nancy a big hug.

Nancy got out of the car. Bess and George were waiting by the theater entrance. They had already bought sodas and popcorn.

"Hurray!" George shouted.

"Nancy, you're amazing!" Bess said.

The girls rushed through the lobby and into the packed theater. As they glanced around for seats, a cheer went up.

"There they are! Way to go, Nancy!"

Nancy, Bess, and George hurried down the center aisle toward the cheering group.

"We saved seats for you," Jenny said.

"I'm glad you made it," Nina said.

The three latecomers sat down. Nancy took the aisle seat. Jason and Mike were sitting behind her. Behind them sat Brenda.

"So how did you crack the case?" Jason asked. "Or is it a detective's secret?"

"I'll tell you one thing," Nancy said. "What you said about stacks of notebooks at the Bell gave me a clue I needed."

"I don't get it," Jason said.

"Maybe I'll explain later," Nancy said.

Brenda leaned forward. "I need a

73

new interview now. How about after the movie?"

Before Nancy could answer, the lights dimmed. She sat back in her seat. Someone tapped her on the shoulder. It was Jason. He handed her his blue notebook.

"You might as well take this," he said. "I don't know how to use it. And by the way, you're pretty good."

"Only pretty good?" Nancy asked.

"Well, *really* pretty good," Jason said.

"Really pretty good?" Nancy asked. "Come on, Jason. Say it."

"Okay, okay," Jason said. "You're the best detective—for now."

As the theme music for *Star Quest 2* began, Nancy knelt by the small aisle light. She opened her own notebook and wrote:

It's great to write in this notebook again. I found the missing *Star Quest 2* passes for my friends and me. Jason found out something, too.

A notebook can't make you into a good detective—just the way a bat can't make you into a good ball-player. You have to practice. I hope I get lots more practice solving mysteries. I even have a second notebook ready for the day when this one fills up! Case closed.